From my home to yours — M.R.

For Skye — E.H.

BLOOMSBURY CHILDREN'S BOOKS
Bloomsbury Publishing Plc
50 Bedford Square, London, WC1B 3DP, UK
29 Earlsfort Terrace, Dublin 2, Ireland

BLOOMSBURY, BLOOMSBURY CHILDREN'S BOOKS and the Diana logo are trademarks of Bloomsbury Publishing Plc

First published in Great Britain 2020 by Bloomsbury Publishing Plc

Text copyright © Michelle Robinson, 2020
Illustrations copyright © Emily Hamilton, 2020

Michelle Robinson and Emily Hamilton have asserted their rights under the Copyright, Designs and Patents Act, 1988,
to be identified as the Author and Illustrator of this work

A catalogue record for this book is available from the British Library

ISBN: 978 1 5266 2981 4 (HB)
ISBN: 978 1 5266 2980 7 (PB)
ISBN: 978 1 5266 2982 1 (eBook)

5 7 9 10 8 6

Printed and bound in the United Kingdom by Bell and Bain Ltd, Glasgow

All papers used by Bloomsbury Publishing Plc are natural, recyclable products from wood grown in well managed forests.
The manufacturing processes conform to the environmental regulations of the country of origin.

To find out more about our authors and books visit www.bloomsbury.com and sign up for our newsletters

The Save the Children Fund is a charity registered in
England and Wales (213890) and Scotland (SC039570).

FSC
www.fsc.org

MIX
Paper from
responsible sources
FSC® C007785

The World Made a RAINBOW

Written by
Michelle Robinson

Illustrated by
Emily Hamilton

BLOOMSBURY
CHILDREN'S BOOKS
LONDON OXFORD NEW YORK NEW DELHI SYDNEY

All of the world had to stay home today.
I wished that it didn't. I wanted to play.

I missed everybody. My Grandma. My friends.
My mum said, "You'll see them, once everything mends."

"Let's paint a **big rainbow** to put on display.
When people pass by it and see it, they'll say,
'*All rainstorms must end,
and this rainstorm will, too.*'"

"And they'll feel a bit happier, all thanks to you."

So we dig out the paint pots.

I LOVE
making
ART!

We've got lots of RED
so I make a good start.

But RED makes me think of
the chairs in my class . . .

Mum gives me a cuddle,
"This rainstorm will pass."

"I can't reach the ORANGE . . .!"
But mum has to work,
And dad's with my brother,
who's going berserk.

I'll start on the YELLOW. It's bright like the sun.
I splodge it around with the red.

It's good FUN!

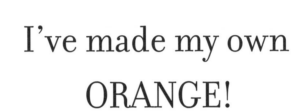

I've made my own
ORANGE!

But I can't make GREEN.
I'd need BLUE for that,
and the blue pot's wiped clean.

I start to feel lonely.

I start to feel sad.

Then . . .

"How about odd bits
of cardboard?" says dad.

He cuts, and I stick,
and my brother helps, too.
We have to mix flour and water for glue.

It looks really good . . .

"Like the ocean," says mum.
"And all the **adventures** we've still got to come . . ."

"The forest!"

"The park!"

"The **light** couldn't SHINE if it never knew dark."

"And **rainbows** can't COLOUR the world without **rain**."

So we get back to work on my rainbow again.

I've never been quite sure what INDIGO's like?
Dad laughs. "INDIGO —
like your very first bike!"

And they dig out a memory box I've never seen,
Packed with mementoes
from places we've been.

I shout, "Indigo!"
    as I spot my mum's jeans.
Well, I can't cut *them* out —
    so we use magazines.

Then Dad takes a snapshot for Gran, and I say,
    "Memories are good.
        We'll make more every day."

My rainbow looks GREAT!

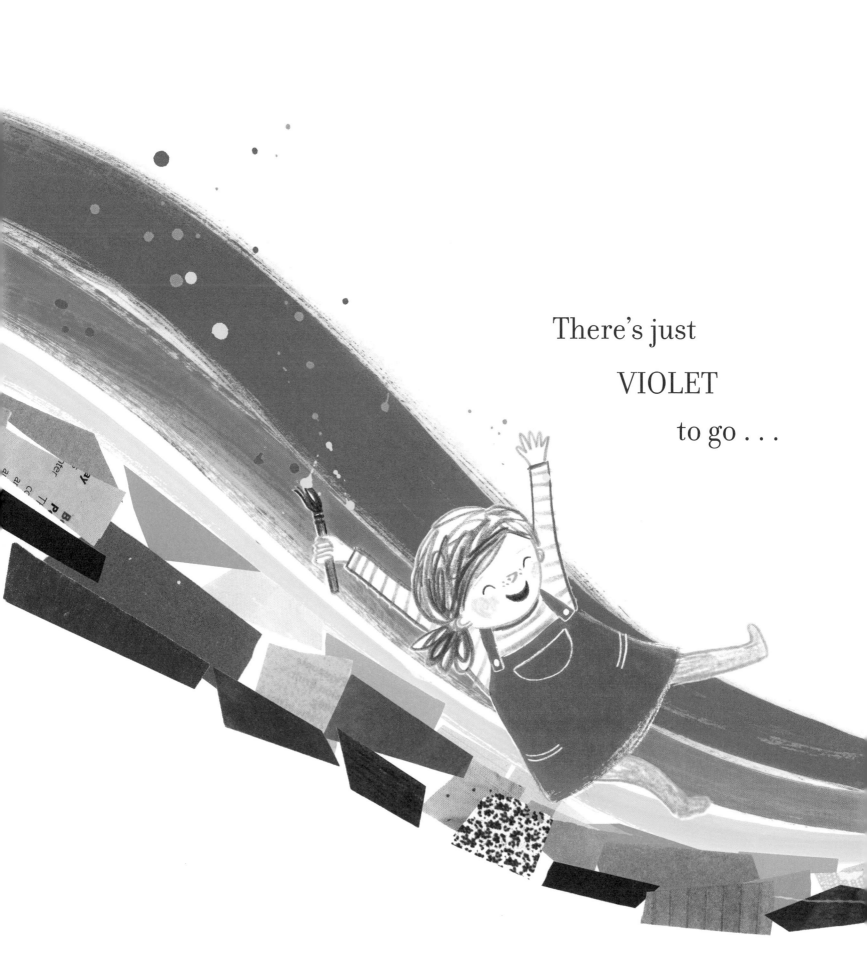

There's just

VIOLET

to go . . .

Violet, the **loveliest** person I know!

Violet's my best friend.
I miss her,
SO much.

Mum fetches her laptop.
"Let's put you in touch . . ."

And — would you believe?

Violet feels just like me —

And she's making a rainbow for people to see!

We walk to see hers,

and she walks to see mine.

We wave to each other and really, it's fine.

Not perfect — but neither's my rainbow. So what?
I'm perfectly **happy** with all that I've got.

Violet, my parents, my brother, my friends . . .

And we'll still have **each other**
when this rainstorm ends!

Save the Children

Save the Children exists to help every child be who they want to be.
We find new ways to reach children who need us most,
no matter where they're growing up.

Now the coronavirus crisis has made the world even more unfair.
Societies are in disarray. This is our once-in-a-lifetime chance
to break the old rules and write new ones. To make the world
better for children and change the future.

www.savethechildren.org.uk